PROFESSOR I.Q. EXPLORES THE BRAIN

by Seymour Simon

illustrated by Dennis Kendrick

PROFESSOR I.Q. EXPLORES THE BRAIN

by Seymour Simon

illustrated by Dennis Kendrick

Published by Bell Books
Boyds Mills Press, Inc.
A Highlights Company
910 Church Street
Honesdale, Pennsylvania 18431

Publisher Cataloging-in-Publication Data
Simon, Seymour.
Professor I.Q. explores the brain / by Seymour Simon ; illustrated by Dennis Kendrick.
[48]p. : col. ill. ; cm.
Summary: Easy-to-understand text for the beginning reader.
ISBN 1-878093-27-4
1. Brain—Juvenile literature.   [1. Brain.]   I. Kendrick, Dennis, ill.   II. Title.
612.82—dc20   1993
Library of Congress Catalog Card Number: 91-77612

First edition, 1993
Some of the material in this book appeared in a different form
under the title *About Your Brain,* published by McGraw-Hill.
Book designed by Kathleen Westray
The text of this book is set in 14-point Optima and Palatino.
The illustrations are done in pen and ink and watercolors.
Distributed by St. Martin's Press
Printed in Hong Kong

10 9 8 7 6 5 4 3 2 1

For Michael and Debra—long life
—S.S.

To Andy with love
—D.K.

You probably have used a computer in school or at home.
Computers are amazing machines.
They can keep careful records and do long calculations very quickly and accurately.
They can correct your spelling and find any fact in an encyclopedia in an instant.
Computers can play games with you and help you learn all kinds of subjects.
Computers can help people fly airplanes, take photographs, run machines, send satellites around the Earth, and look inside a human body.
Computers can do lots of different things.
But human brains made computers.
And human brains are more wonderful than any computer.

An adult brain weighs about
3 pounds (1-and-1/2 kilograms) and uses
only 10 or 12 watts of electricity.
Yet that small organ in your head can
do many more jobs than the biggest and
fastest computer ever made.
Your brain directs and controls all the
muscles and organs in your body.
It receives messages from your eyes,
ears, nose, tongue, and skin and makes
sense of the world around you.
It stores information in your memory.
It is involved in everything you do,
from eating and growing,
to running and sleeping,
to breathing and thinking.

Although your brain makes up only
2 percent of your body's weight, it needs
20 percent of your body's oxygen.
It needs oxygen day and night, because
even when you sleep your brain is busy
at work sometimes dreaming,

but always keeping your heart beating,
your lungs breathing,
your muscles moving.
If the supply of oxygen to your brain
stops for just 10 seconds you will
lose consciousness.

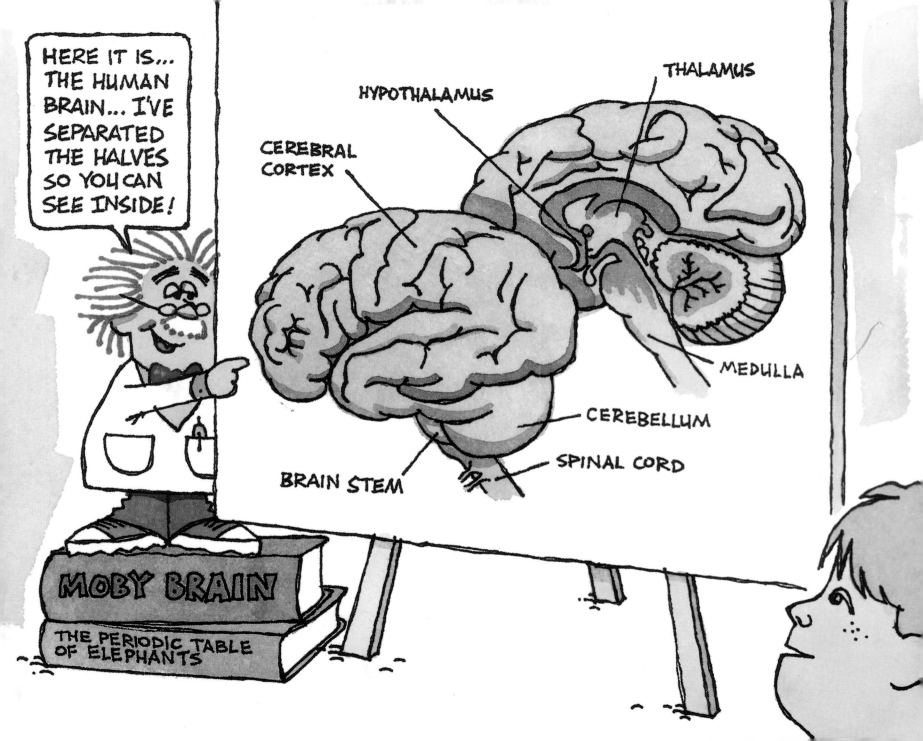

A human brain is made up of 50 - 100 billion tiny nerve cells, called **neurons**. That's about the same amount as the number of stars in the Milky Way Galaxy. There are ten times that number of **glial** cells in the brain, which surround, support, and nourish the neurons. Each neuron can carry electrical and chemical signals. An electrical signal flashes down a neuron. When it reaches the end of the neuron, the signal triggers the release of certain chemicals.

The chemicals reach other nearby neurons and trigger them into sending signals. In this way, signals can travel back and forth across the brain in a tiny fraction of a second. No neuron works just by itself. Each neuron connects with many other neurons in your brain and all over your body. The place where a nerve impulse travels from one neuron to another is called a **synapse.**
Groups of neurons in your brain seem to have certain jobs.

Thousands take part in even the simplest actions, such as moving your fingers or turning your head.

Millions of signals flash through your brain every moment of your life.

They bring information about your insides: your heartbeat, your breathing, your temperature, and other body processes outside your awareness.

They bring news about an itch in your nose, the sound of a song on a radio, the smell of an apple.

Inside your brain, millions of other signals work on the incoming information and produce memories, thoughts, emotions, and plans on what to do next.

Signals are sent out from your brain to scratch your itchy nose, change the radio station, bite the apple.

Meanwhile your brain is also sending out commands to keep your body functioning at its best.

Each task uses several different regions of your brain.

Anatomy Made Simple!

IMPROVE YOUR I.Q.

ABC's of Brain Surgery

BODY SENSE, BODY NON-SENSE
S. SIMON

(YOUR MESSAGE HERE)

PUSS 'N' BOOTS

OF MICE & MEN

Using special instruments such as X-rays and scanners, scientists have mapped and explored the different regions of the brain. They've learned many things about the regions and what each does. But no one knows how memories are stored in the brain. No one knows how we think. No one knows how everything in the brain works. Nor does anyone know all the ways in which the regions of the brain work together.

Try This...

Look at your head in a mirror.
Use your hands to feel the way your head curves.
You are feeling the bony armor called the skull
that surrounds your brain.
Your skull is made up of 28 bones, 8 of which
form the egg-shaped cradle of the brain called
the cranium.
The other 20 bones form and shape your face,
jaws, and inner ears.
Openings in the skull allow passage to nerves
and blood vessels.
Your brain is about the size of a large grapefruit.
It looks like a wrinkled blob of pinkish-gray jelly.
Your brain sits in a kind of fluid bath of chemicals
in your skull.
The bony skull and the fluid inside help protect
and cushion your brain from shocks.

LAB
SWEET
LAB

The largest part of your brain is called the **cerebrum**. Cerebrum comes from a Latin word that means "brain." Your cerebrum fills the whole upper part of your skull.

The deeply wrinkled surface of your cerebrum is called the **cerebral cortex**. Cortex comes from a word that means "bark," so cerebral cortex means "brain bark."

The cortex covers the cerebrum like bark covers a tree.

CEREBRAL CORTEX

☆ ☆ EXTRA ☆ ☆

PROFESSOR I.Q. MAKES AMAZING NEW DISCOVERY!

$$E \equiv mC^3$$

Physicist's Relativity Theory Helps Explain the Universe

The "Prof"

Try This...

Spread out a newspaper page. If the wrinkled cortex were smoothed out, it would take up about as much space as the page. Although the cortex is only about 1/8-inch thick, it contains 3/4 of all the brain's neurons.

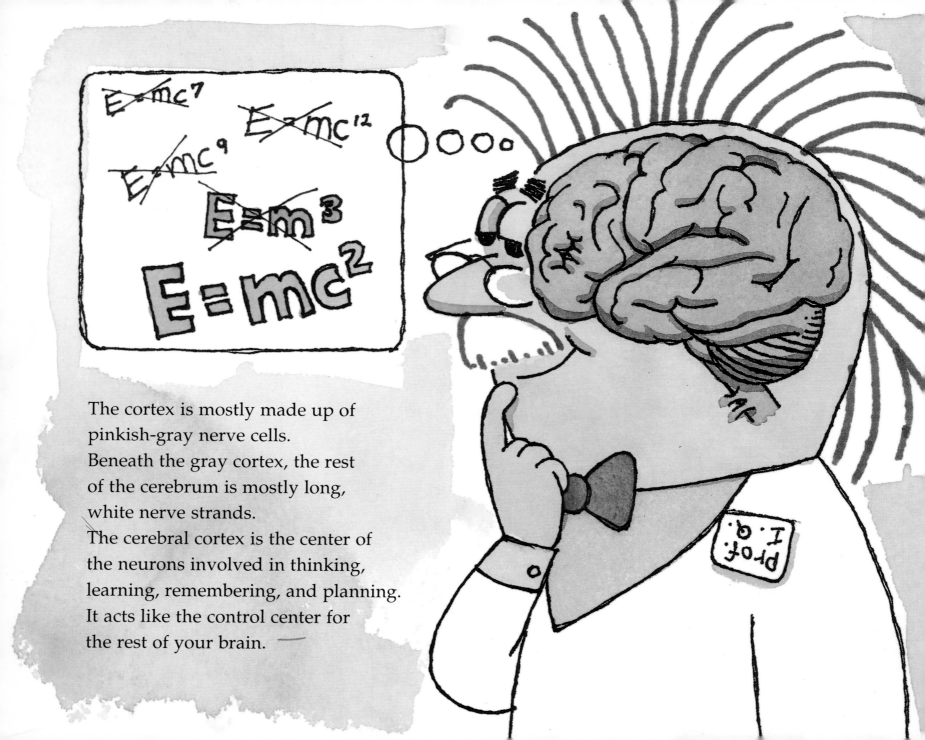

The cortex is mostly made up of pinkish-gray nerve cells. Beneath the gray cortex, the rest of the cerebrum is mostly long, white nerve strands. The cerebral cortex is the center of the neurons involved in thinking, learning, remembering, and planning. It acts like the control center for the rest of your brain.

Try This...

Try to memorize these words in one minute:

cat sky ask wet tin pen run ball

Now close the book and write down all the words.

Check to see how many you remembered.

Trying to remember something puts your cerebrum in action.

Now, Try This...

Use your finger or the back of a pen or pencil to find your way out of this maze.
Once again, your cerebrum is in action.

The cerebrum is the region of the brain
most in action when you read a book,
hear music,
taste a peanut butter and jelly sandwich,
smell a flower,
or touch an ice cube.
It's most in action when you play chess,
watch television,
remember the way home,
or tell a story.

The main difference between the
brains of humans and other animals
is in the cerebrum.
Fishes and frogs have a very small cerebrum.
Reptiles and birds have a slightly larger
cerebrum, and the beginnings of a cortex.
Mammals such as apes and whales
have the largest cerebrums.
And humans have the most developed
cerebrums among mammals and the
largest for their body weight.

ONCE UPON A TIME-SPACE CONTINUUM...

HOME
HOME
Home
HOME
HOME

Try This....

Your cerebrum and its cortex are divided into two halves, or **cerebral hemispheres**. Each hemisphere is almost a mirror image of the other. You can trace the line between the hemispheres by running your finger between your eyes, across the top of your head, and down towards your neck.

The two hemispheres of your brain are connected to each other by a thick bundle of nerves so that your actions are coordinated. Though both sides of your brain look alike, they are not the same.
One side of your brain is dominant, and takes control over the other side.
For right-sided people, the left side of the brain takes control.
For left-sided people, the right side of the brain takes control.

Your ability to use language is located most often in the left hemisphere.

In most people, the left hemisphere also controls mathematics and other kinds of logical thinking, while the right hemisphere seems to control special artistic talents and emotional qualities.

Your senses have centers in both hemispheres.

For example, images that enter your eyes from the right are given meaning by a small area in the left side of your brain.

Sounds that enter your ears from the left are given meaning by a small area in the right side of your brain.

Muscles on each side of your body are controlled by the opposite side of your brain.

For example, your right hemisphere controls your left leg, left arm, and left facial muscles.

That's why damage to the brain's right side sometimes results in paralysis of muscles on the body's left side.

ARE YOU RIGHT-BRAINED OR LEFT-BRAINED?

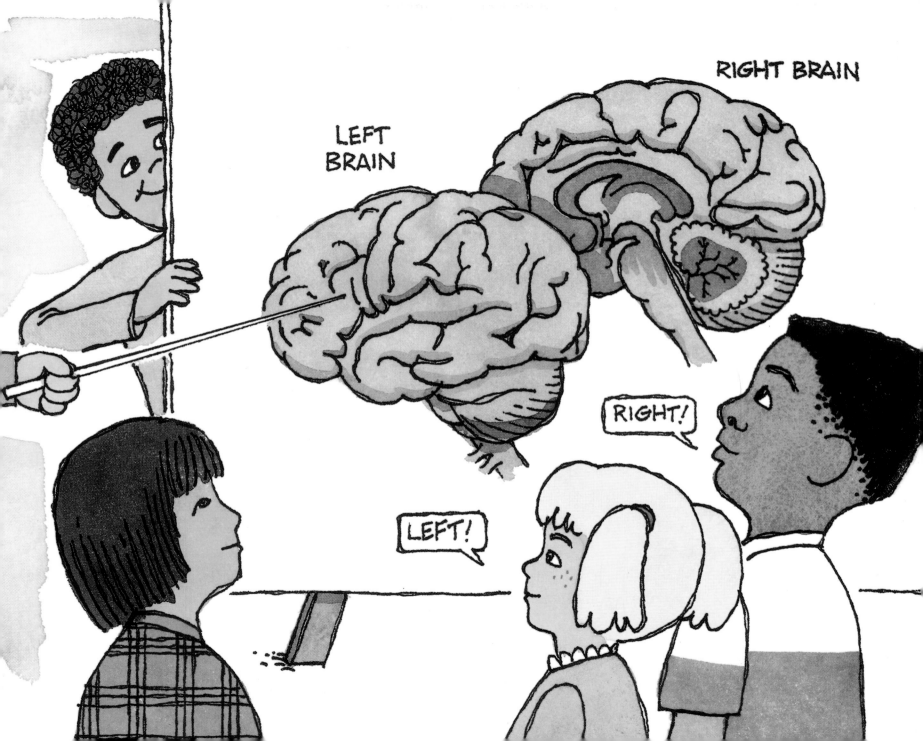

Some scientists have used a tiny electric needle to help explore the cerebral cortex. They can do this because the brain itself does not have any pain-sensing nerves. The needle gives a small electric charge to a single spot in the brain.

A touch of the charge in different spots can make the person move a finger,

or move a toe,

or open his mouth.

A touch in other spots can make the person hear a bell,

or see a light,

or feel hot,

even though none of these things are present.

But there are some areas of the cortex that seem to show no such response. Once they were thought of as silent areas. But now they are thought of as association areas.

That's where different kinds of information from all the senses come together.

Many scientists think that memory and thinking take place mainly in the association areas.

But no one is really sure of that.

Scientists use a special instrument to look at "brain waves," the electrical activities of the brain. The instrument is called an electroencephalograph, or EEG. The EEG prints out brain waves to show what happens when a person is awake or asleep.

When you fall asleep, the cortex works more slowly than when you are awake. When you are in the lightest part of sleep, you often dream and your brain waves change.

This phase of sleep is called R.E.M. (rapid eye movement), because during it your eyes move back and forth rapidly under your eyelids.

$E = mc^2$

The square of the hypotenuse is equal to the sum of the remaining two sides.

Another part of your brain is called the **cerebellum**.
The cerebellum helps your voluntary muscles work
together smoothly and helps maintain balance.
The cerebellum allows you to walk or run easily,
to play ball or dance gracefully,
to drink water without making a mess.

H₂O

I GOT IT, I GOT IT!

Try This...
The cerebellum is located at the back and lower part
of the brain underneath the cerebrum.
Place your fingers just above the back of your neck.
The cerebellum is just beneath your fingers.
It looks like a little wrinkled golf ball.
The word cerebellum comes from Latin and means
"little brain."
Acting as a message passageway between the
cerebellum and the cerebrum is a band of nerve fibers
called the **pons**.

CEREBELLUM

Dear Mom,

When you try a new sport or a new dance, you may be very clumsy at first.
But as you practice, you begin to do things in the right way without thinking about them.
You might say that you "have the feel" of the game.
That's because your cerebellum is now using memories of previously learned movements to help in controlling or directing your muscles.
The cerebellum constantly receives messages from the muscles and joints in your body.
Large neurons in the cerebellum "map" the position of your head, neck, feet, arms, and trunk so it can tell each body part where it is and what it has to do to keep going.
The cerebrum, the "thinking" part of your brain, makes fine adjustments to the actions of your cerebellum.
That helps you to shoot a basketball, write a letter, or play a tune on a musical instrument.

The cerebellum lets you do lots of things without your really thinking about them.
It helps you to walk while you're talking to a friend.
It helps you to eat while you're reading a book.

It helps you to skip rope or dance while you're singing a song.

Deep inside the hemispheres of the cerebrum is another part of your brain called the **thalamus**.
The thalamus is a bit smaller than the cerebellum.
Thalamus means "inner room" in Latin. The thalamus is the part of your brain that first receives messages from your body about heat and cold, pain and pressure, smell and taste.
But the thalamus cannot tell exactly where in your body these sensations come from. It also cannot tell exactly what it is that is causing these sensations.

The thalamus does other things as well.
It seems to regulate your cycles of sleep and wakefulness.
It seems to direct the way you sometimes "feel good" or "feel awful."

Feel Good

Feel Awful

Try This...

Suppose you touch an ice cube or feel a pin with your finger.
The thalamus makes you aware of a feeling of cold or pain somewhere at the end of your arm.
But before you know that the feeling is in a finger and that it is caused by ice or a pointy object, messages speed from the thalamus to the sensory parts of the cerebral cortex.
The thalamus is also connected to the optic nerve (from your eyes) and acts like a kind of relay station for sensory messages from the body.

Below the thalamus is another very small part of the brain called the **hypothalamus.**

"Hypo" means "under" so hypothalamus means "under the inner room."

The hypothalamus is only about the size of a lima bean. Yet it is the control center for some of your most powerful feelings and drives.

In one experiment, a scientist sent small electric charges into a part of the hypothalamus of an animal.
The scientist discovered that the charge turned a

The Many FACES of HYPO CAT

MEOW!

Furious

Friendly

Hungry

quiet cat into a hissing bundle of scratching fury that would attack anything in sight.

But the instant that the current was switched off, the cat became as friendly as before.

Sending a small electric current into a different part of the hypothalamus made the cat hungry.

No matter how much food the cat ate, it would continue to stuff itself until the current was shut off.

Other experiments with the hypothalamus showed that an electric current in different parts could trigger fear, thirst, worry, or tiredness.

IT'S **HYP**othalamus, NOT **HIPP**othalamus!

| Fear | Thirst | Worry | Tiredness |

DANGER

PALMS

OTHER STUFF

Besides being important in feeling all kinds of emotions, the hypothalamus performs other tasks as well.

It helps regulate your body's temperature and keeps it constant regardless of how hot or cold your surroundings.

When your body becomes overheated, the hypothalamus stimulates your sweat glands to produce perspiration which comes through the pores and evaporates to cool your skin.

In times of danger or alarm, it prepares your body to flee or to defend yourself. When your heart starts to pound and your palms begin to sweat, your hypothalamus is most in action.

NO MACHINE CAN BEAT THE HUMAN BRAIN... I OUGHT TO KNOW...I OWN ONE!

Between the thalamus and the hypothalamus lies another part of your brain called the **brainstem.** The brainstem is the widened top of the spinal cord. In humans the brainstem is about three inches long. From the brainstem, the brain swells outward like a flower opening on a plant stem.

In animals such as fishes and reptiles, the brainstem makes up much of the brain. One important part of the brainstem is named the **medulla.** It controls many basic life functions such as breathing, digestion, blood pressure, swallowing, and heart rate. Quick, simple reactions of your body called **reflexes** often act through the medulla.

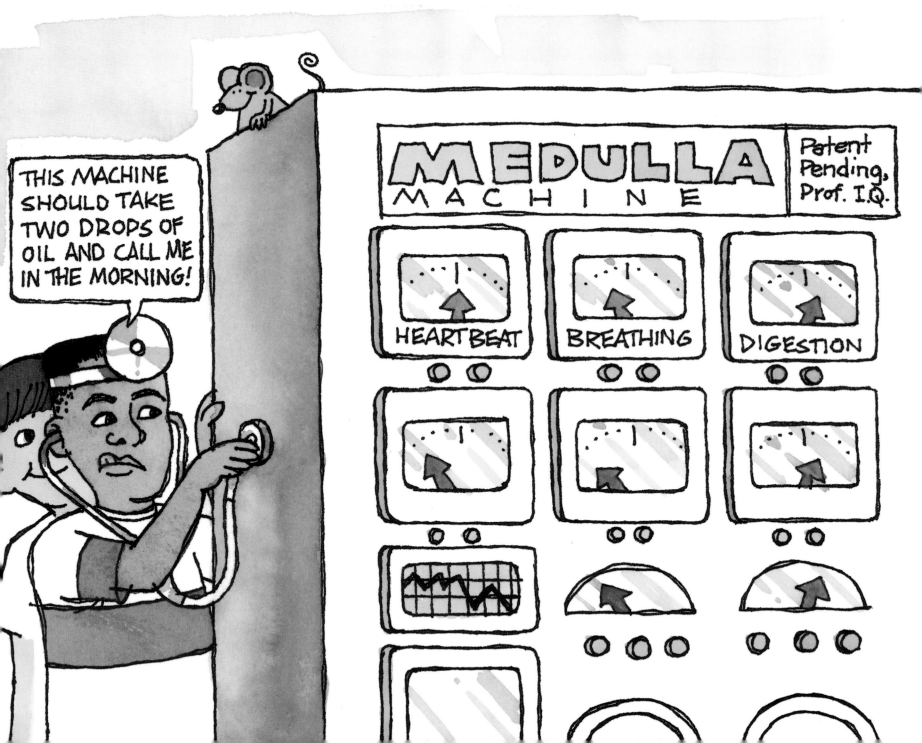

Here is a way to show a simple reflex in action.
You will need the help of a friend, a piece of clear, stiff plastic, and a sheet of paper.
Ask your friend to hold the plastic in front of her face and look straight ahead without moving.
Crumple the paper into a ball and throw it at the plastic.
Watch your friend blink her eyelids.
Even if she tries not to blink at the paper, she probably will not be able to stop.
Blinking is a simple reflex controlled in large part by the medulla.

Here's another simple reflex you can watch.
It's called the pupillary reflex.
You need to look at the dark spot in your friend's eye, called the pupil.
Have your friend stay in a dark room for a few minutes.
Then snap on the light in the room.
Watch the pupil in your friend's eye suddenly shrink in size.

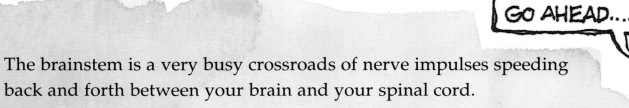

GO AHEAD....

The brainstem is a very busy crossroads of nerve impulses speeding back and forth between your brain and your spinal cord.
Spread through the brainstem is a net-like collection of special nerve cells.
These nerve cells act like a kind of filter.
They determine which messages will be let through to the higher centers of the brain.

Try This...

BANG! R-R-RING! ARF!

List all the different things that you can sense around you this very minute.
You can see this page, your fingers, the room you are in.
You can hear all kinds of noises around you.
You can feel the pressure of your shoes and your clothing and the position of your body.
You can feel your tongue in your mouth and a breeze on your skin.
If you were to think about everything that you see, feel, hear, and smell, you would be overwhelmed.
The net-like nerve cells in your brainstem let only some of the messages through.
This lets you concentrate on some signals and pay no attention to others.

Below your brainstem is the rest of your spinal cord.

The spinal cord is the main nerve pathway between your body and your brain.

The top of the spinal cord, the brainstem, is about as thick as your thumb.

About 18 inches below your brain, the spinal cord ends as a thin thread.

From your spinal cord, 31 pairs of nerves branch out to all parts of your body.

Try This...

Reach behind yourself and run your fingers
down the center of your back.
Your backbone feels like one spool of thread
atop another.
It helps protect your spinal cord from injury,
just as your skull helps protect your brain.
The spinal cord is also bathed in the same kind
of fluid that surrounds your brain.
The spinal cord is made of nerve cells and looks
much like the brain.
Parts are gray and parts are white.

NO PEDDLERS

Fishes, frogs, snakes, birds, and mammals all have backbones and spinal cords. We call animals with backbones, **vertebrates**.

Worms, clams, lobsters, and insects do not have backbones or spinal cords. We call animals without backbones, **invertebrates.**

Your spinal cord and your brain make up your **central nervous system**.
Let's follow your central nervous system in action. Here are just a few of the things that happened when you saw this book:
First of all, you thought of picking up the book and reading it.
Messages shot back and forth across your cerebral cortex.
Finally, you came to a decision.
The part of the cortex that controls movement sent out messages to the cerebellum.
The cerebellum sent back messages that gave the location of your arms, legs, head, and other body parts.
The cortex then sent out signals for certain muscles to move in certain ways.
The signals traveled down your spinal cord and through nerves to muscles in your arms.

You picked up the book and opened it.
Your eyes moved back and forth across each line.
Light patterns entered your eyes and triggered nerve messages.
The messages traveled through a nerve and then to that part of the cortex that takes care of seeing.
Then the messages of the light patterns were recognized as words and sentences.
Other parts of the cortex thought about what the words meant.
Your memory stored some of the information for later use.
All this time, the medulla was keeping track of your heartbeat and your breathing.
Your brainstem was filtering out other messages that were not important.
And all of this was taking place in split seconds.

HMMM, I THINK I'LL WRITE A BOOK ALL ABOUT MY OWN BRAIN...

BUT WHAT WILL YOU DO WHEN YOU GET TO PAGE TWO?

We know so much about the brain, yet so much remains to be found out.

THESE EXPERIMENTS ARE MY FAVORITE PARTS OF THIS BOOK!

Try This...

Try to balance a broom handle on your right forefinger and speak at the same time. Now try to balance it on your left forefinger and speak. For some reason, it is easier to do this with your left finger than with your right one.

Press one of your fingers against your closed eyelid. You not only feel the pressure, but also see a flash of light.

Gently press a pencil point into the back of your hand.
You may feel a sensation of cold rather than the pressing point.

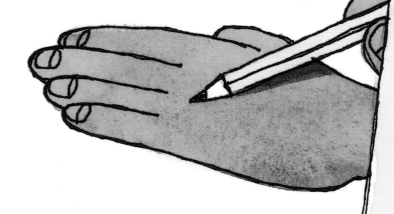

BRRRRRRR !!!

Your brain and spinal cord take part in everything you do.
Your brain is the most complex organ in your body.
In more important ways than the color of your skin or hair,
or how your face looks, or how tall you are,
your brain is really what makes you, *you*.

Seymour Simon has written more than one hundred highly acclaimed science books for young readers, many of which have been selected by the National Science Teachers Association as Outstanding Science Trade Books for Children. He lives in Great Neck, New York.

Dennis Kendrick has illustrated many books for children, a number of them in collaboration with Seymour Simon. His titles include THE SANDLOT, MONSTER BIRTHDAY, and STORIES ABOUT ROSIE. He lives in New York City.